# The day the
## guinea pig talked

# The day the guinea pig talked

by

## PAUL GALLICO

Illustrated by
**DULAC**

DOUBLEDAY & COMPANY, INC. GARDEN CITY, NEW YORK

To
Sarah
More

Library of Congress Catalog Card Number 64-11181
Copyright © 1963 by Paul Gallico
Copyright © 1963 by Mathemata A. G.
Illustrations Copyright © 1963 by William Heinemann Ltd.
All Rights Reserved
Printed in the United States of America
First Edition in the United States of America

IN THEIR SECRET PLACE, down in the cellar in the old stone house, Cecile and Jean-Pierre looked at one another.

Cecile said, 'Jean-Pierre, how I wish you could understand me!'

Jean-Pierre said, 'Oh, Cecile, how I wish you could understand me!'

And both of them said, 'I wish, I wish, I wish you could.'

But they couldn't, for Jean-Pierre was a Guinea Pig. He was a year old and quite clever, but he only spoke Guinea Pig Talk.

Cecile was a little girl. She was eight years old and tall for her age. But Cecile could only speak French, for she *was* French and lived with her father and mother on a farm in the South of France, on a hill behind the city of Cannes.

Jean-Pierre, of course, is French for John-Peter. Cecile had called him that because it seemed a nice name to her. Jean-Pierre liked it. All the other Guinea Pigs he knew had only one name. He had two. He knew that his name was Jean-Pierre and Cecile's name was Cecile. But that was all that he could understand.

Every evening, after Cecile fed him in their secret place in the cellar, she would talk to him in French and he would speak to her in Guinea Pig Talk, and after a while they would just look at one another and wish that they could understand.

For Jean-Pierre had so much to say to Cecile.

And Cecile had so many, many things she wanted to tell Jean-Pierre.

Each was most curious about what the other was thinking.

There seemed to be no way for them ever to find out.

On the farm where Cecile lived was a dog named Bobi, and a cat named Coco and a rabbit named Gris-Gris. Bobi was rather a long yellow dog with a long yellow tail but he had a

nice smile. Coco was black with three white feet. Gris-Gris was gray and cuddly but very stupid.

Cecile was fond of them but most of all she cared about Jean-Pierre, because he was her very own. Bobi belonged to her in a way and so did Coco and Gris-Gris, but Jean-Pierre belonged to her most of all because she had bought him with her own pocket-money from a pet shop in Cannes. He cost five francs. She had been saving up this money to buy a skipping-rope.

Five francs in French money is the same thing as ten dimes. Ten dimes is not much if you have hundreds of billions of dimes or even millions, but if ten dimes are the only dimes you have and you need them to buy a skipping-rope, it is the most money in the world.

Cecile went to school in Cannes which was five miles from the farm. Her mother took her there every morning on the bus and called for her every afternoon.

From the bus stop it was only a short walk to the school and on the way they had to pass the pet shop.

They passed it going in the morning and they passed it coming back in the afternoon.

One day, Cecile saw Jean-Pierre in the window in a cage with eight other Guinea Pigs. The cage was on a shelf, just high enough to let Cecile look into the faces of the Guinea Pigs when she passed. And of course, if they wanted to, the Guinea Pigs could look into hers.

The other eight Guinea Pigs took no notice at all when Cecile went past. They went on munching their lettuce leaves, or sleeping in little heaps in a corner, so that you could not tell where one began and the other left off.

But Jean-Pierre (though at that time he was not known as Jean-Pierre, since he did not yet belong to anyone and had no name) always looked up at Cecile in the strangest way.

It was the kind of look which meant there was something on the tip of his tongue he wanted to say to her.

He was different from the other Guinea Pigs because he came all the way from Abyssinia. Abyssinia is in Africa. His fur was long and rough instead of short and smooth like ordinary Guinea Pigs. His color was rather like a frying-pan which had been left out in the rain and had gone rusty. Thus, while he was mostly black, it was not a real proper black but more of a browny-black. Only his ears were much lighter and so fine you could almost see right through them. His nose was pink and so were his feet. His whiskers were white and very clean, because he kept them that way. But his eyes were golden.

The eyes of all the other Guinea Pigs were either black like beads, or brown like coffee beans. Only the eyes of Jean-Pierre were golden, and his fur rough instead of smooth.

Cecile saw at once that Jean-Pierre was a very special Guinea Pig.

Jean-Pierre noticed Cecile the very first time she went by the window, after their cage had been put there. But, of course, then he did not know that her name was Cecile.

He only knew he liked her.

She was not as pretty as some of the other little girls who went past the window, but it didn't matter. Her hair was so browny brown that it was almost black. Her skin was brown too, from the sun. Her nose turned up a little and was covered with freckles. Her teeth were white and even, but two of them in front were missing, as is usual with little girls that age. Only her eyes were not like those of anyone else he had ever seen. They were neither blue nor brown nor even green. They were gray.

And the very first time that she stopped to look into the window as she passed, it seemed to Jean-Pierre as though there was something on the tip of her tongue she wanted to say to him too. He wondered what it was.

Thereafter, every morning and every afternoon, each time Cecile and her mother went by, Cecile would stop to look at Jean-Pierre.

And Jean-Pierre would also pause at whatever he was doing, which might be gnawing at the core of an apple, or tidying up his fur, or even scratching himself. Then he would come over to the window and look at Cecile.

Later, at home, when she was not busy with her lessons, but mostly at night when she was alone in bed, she thought about Jean-Pierre. For by this time, that was the name she had given him.

She wondered why his eyes were golden. She wondered why he was so special and different.

She could hardly wait for each new morning when she would pass the shop where she would be able to see him again.

Jean-Pierre was feeling exactly the same.

When he was not busy eating, or tidying his fur and whiskers, but mostly at night when he joined a heap of his friends in the corner, and just before he went to sleep, he thought about the little girl with the brown face.

He wondered why her eyes were gray and so very clear, not like the eyes of other people. He wondered why she was so special.

He could hardly wait for each new morning when she would pass the shop and he could see her again.

One day, Cecile's mother asked her, 'Must you stop every time we go past here? What is it you are staring at?' For the window of the pet shop was full of all kinds of other little animals as well as Guinea Pigs. There were puppies and kittens and turtles and goldfish and canaries, a parrot and even a monkey.

Cecile had replied, 'Can't you see? It's Jean-Pierre,' and she pointed to him as he came over to the window and looked at her.

Cecile's mother smiled. 'How do you know he is called Jean-Pierre?' she asked.

'Because that is what I have named him,' Cecile replied.

Sometime later Cecile had a terrible fright.

When she passed the window of the shop, she saw there were only seven Guinea Pigs, where before there had always been nine. Someone had bought two.

Cecile cried, 'Oh, Mummy,' (in French, of course) and caught at her mother's arm. 'What if one of them were to be Jean-Pierre?'

Luckily, Jean-Pierre was still there and he came over at once to see her.

And while it did not show, Jean-Pierre was feeling very pale and frightened himself.

A hand had reached into the cage and taken out two of his friends, and they never came back. From then on, whenever anyone came into the shop, Jean-Pierre hid beneath the heap of the other Guinea Pigs.

But Cecile decided that day that she must buy Jean-Pierre.

When her mother learned this, she said, 'Oh dear, Cecile. Haven't we enough pets already without another? We have Bobi and Coco and Gris-Gris.'

'But they aren't really mine,' Cecile cried. 'They just live with us.' Because, of course, every farm has a dog and a cat and at least one rabbit.

Cecile's mother said, 'You will have to pay for him yourself then, out of your own pocket-money. Do you really want him that badly?'

Cecile did not reply, but only nodded her head to say yes. She could not tell her mother why it was she wanted Jean-Pierre so much. During all the days she had been passing by and stopping to look at him, and he at her, something secret had grown up between them. Something shared. Something that made them feel that they belonged to one another. But neither knew what it was, only that they wanted to be together.

8

That day at school, Cecile's teacher had to speak to her twice for not paying attention.

Indeed, it was only too true. Cecile was not listening. She was thinking about Jean-Pierre and whether she had enough money in her little wooden box at home to pay for him. For she had no idea how much a Guinea Pig might cost.

That evening, when she got home, she took all of the pocket-money she had saved up, out of the little wooden box. She counted it three times, and then once more, just in *case* she had made a mistake, and then tied it up in her handkerchief, for she had no purse.

At last, next afternoon when they came from school, Cecile and her mother went into the pet shop to enquire the price of the Guinea Pig.

The woman in charge of the shop told them, most politely, that the Guinea Pigs were five francs each.

Her mother asked Cecile, 'Have you five francs?'

Cecile gave a great sigh of relief. She had been so frightened the woman might have said ten francs, or fifty francs, or even one hundred francs. For how could one tell what a very special Guinea Pig like Jean-Pierre might cost?

But five francs, or ten dimes, was exactly what Cecile had. For she had been saving up for a skipping-rope which cost six francs. It cost that much because it was a very special skipping-rope, an English one, which would have enabled her to skip better and faster than anyone else in school.

It is a strange thing to do, when you have been saving up to buy something like a special skipping-rope, to change your mind and buy a very special Guinea Pig instead. But Cecile could not help herself.

For Jean-Pierre had come over and was looking at her out of his golden eyes, as though saying to her, 'Oh, please buy me.'

Which, indeed, *was* exactly what he was saying to her, only not in so many words.

Then, as they stood there looking at one another for a moment, again that strange, secret feeling was shared between them. If only they might understand one another.

Cecile was quite sure then that it was better to have a very special Guinea Pig, rather than a very special, English skipping-rope.

'Five francs each,' the woman repeated, 'and the little girl can choose whichever one she likes.'

Cecile reached into her pocket, took out her handkerchief in which the money was tied, and paid the five francs.

'Now, which one do you want?' the woman asked Cecile.

Cecile did not even have to point. Jean-Pierre was already waiting at the door of the cage, for he was a clever little Guinea Pig. And there was something about the way he sat there looking so eagerly at Cecile, and waiting for her to open the door, that showed he was now a most happy, as well as clever and special, Guinea Pig.

The woman who owned the shop smiled and said to Cecile's mother, 'Why, he acts as though he knows your little girl already.'

Cecile thought to herself a private thought, which was never spoken aloud, because it would not have been polite to have done so. It was: *How very stupid grown-up people can be. They just don't ever know anything!* Of course she and Jean-Pierre knew each other.

She opened the door of his cage and took him into her hand, he was fat, soft, warm, and his little heart seemed to be beating a thousand to the minute with joy and excitement. Cecile held him to her cheek for a moment and then looked into his golden eyes, which were filled with all the things he seemed to be wanting to say to her. But she knew she would have to take him away and to a secret place, where they could be alone, before she would ever be able to find out what it was.

THE FARM ON which Cecile lived with her father and mother was a different kind of farm from any you might have ever known or seen. Cecile's father did not grow wheat, or corn, or oats, or hay. Nor did he raise pigs, or sheep, or cows like other farmers. Instead he grew thousands and thousands of carnations of every color and kind, and thousands upon thousands of roses as well. He also grew geraniums, cyclamens, anemones, gladioli and tiger lilies. It was a flower farm.

True, there was an apple orchard behind the old stone house, and some pear and plum trees, and a long grape arbour leading up to the door of the house. In the autumn, when the grapes were full and heavy and purple, the grape arbour was like a tunnel.

They kept a few chickens on the farm for fresh eggs. There were also some pigeons flying about. And, of course, there was Bobi and Coco and Gris-Gris. But all the rest was flowers.

Instead of fields there were rows and rows of terraces, like huge steps going downhill from the house. Here the flowers

grew, some in the open, some under cover. They began their life snug in glass-houses, in small pots as seedlings, until two tiny green leaves showed above the black earth. Then they were moved to bigger pots and bigger glass-houses, until they were old enough to live outdoors. That was what a flower farm was like.

From the window of her bedroom Cecile looked out onto the rows and rows of flowers. And in the distance was the Mediterranean Sea.

A sea is almost the same as an ocean, though not quite as large. It was blue and sparkling when the sun shone. When there was a storm it was gray and angry.

Life on a flower farm upon a hillside looking down upon a blue sea is wonderful. One cannot only smell the flowers but also see them in all their beautiful colors. There were pink roses, white and red carnations, salmon-colored geraniums, orange tiger-lilies and lavender cyclamens.

This was where Jean-Pierre came to live with Cecile.

15

During the day when Cecile was at school, Jean-Pierre's wooden cage stood in the window of the barn where he could look out across the courtyard, past the well and the little house where the pigeons lived, to the woods on the hill where the pine trees waved their arms and nodded their green heads.

The wind would bring the scent of the flowers to Jean-Pierre. He would sit with his pink nose to the bars of the cage, smelling them. They made his nose twitch. After his nose twitched for a while he would sneeze. He liked sneezing.

But when Cecile came home from school, or on Sundays after she was bathed and dressed, she would go and fetch him and take him to their secret place.

It was down in the cellar of the old stone farmhouse. It was not really and truly secret since everybody knew where it was. But Cecile's mother and father did not often go there and so it was secret enough for Cecile and Jean-Pierre.

One of the reasons that Cecile took Jean-Pierre down there was so that they could be alone together.

For grown-ups would never understand that she and her Guinea Pig had most important things to say to one another. And that someday they even hoped to be able to understand WHAT they were saying.

Some people think that Guinea Pigs do not make any kind of noise. Cecile knew that this was not true. For from the very first moment she had him, Jean-Pierre had been full of sounds.

When she held him close to her ear she could hear him grunt softly almost like a little pig. Well, of course he *was* a Guinea Pig.

Sometimes he would squeal. Or click his teeth together. He could chirrup like a sparrow or croak like a frog. And when he was alarmed he would even give a small shriek.

But all of this was Guinea Pig Talk and Cecile could not understand a word of it. Cecile's dearest wish was that she might

understand what he was saying to her. Sometimes she pretended she did, when she put her ear close to his pink nose and listened to his tiny noises. But she knew it was pretend all the time.

It was the same for Jean-Pierre. For him, Cecile made all kinds of noises too, whispers, shouts and cries, some of which hurt his tender little ears. And at no time could he understand a single thing she was saying. For, of course, it was all human talk and French as well.

Another reason for taking Jean-Pierre down to the secret place was that Cecile fed him there. There was a kind of stone shelf in the cellar, not far from a small electric light globe all covered with dust and cobwebs. It was dark enough to be properly secret, yet light enough to see.

This shelf was most useful in more ways than one. It did not matter if Jean-Pierre made a mess on it, and he usually did when he had his dinner. It was easy to clean, but best of all it was just the right height. When Cecile stood up straight she could rest her chin upon it. Then she and Jean-Pierre could look into one another's faces as they used to do when Cecile passed the pet shop on her way to and from school.

This was important, for when Cecile had to look down upon Jean-Pierre all she could see was his browny back with its black marking somewhat in the shape of a potato.

And when Jean-Pierre had to look up at Cecile, all *he* could see were her legs going up past her knees and into her skirts like two thin tree-trunks.

But when Cecile put Jean-Pierre on the stone shelf in the cellar it was just right. In this way they could look at one another face to face for as long as they liked.

Jean-Pierre's dinner was made up of all kinds of things, some of which Cecile brought down from the kitchen, such as lettuce or cabbage leaf, crumbs of bread or cake and a bit of cheese, and others which were stored in the cellar. These were treats like slices of pumpkin, apples, pears, grapes, or pieces of pomegranate.

Perhaps best of all Jean-Pierre loved pomegranate.

A pomegranate is a fruit which grows in the South of France and other warm countries. It looks like a large red apple and has a hard skin almost like a shell. It is full of small red seeds bursting with sweet juice. The seeds were not only good to eat, but also fun. For when Jean-Pierre bit into them the juice got all over his whiskers and face and then Cecile would have to wipe them with her handkerchief.

While Cecile was busy setting out his dinner, Jean-Pierre would sit up on his hind legs like a squirrel and sniff. His golden eyes rolled from one side to the other as he tried to see what he was going to have. But, of course, the most excitement was when Cecile gave him a piece of pomegranate, which she would save for last.

Cecile would rest her chin upon the edge of the stone shelf and watch him while he ate. Jean-Pierre was a little greedy and never finished what he started. He would have a bit of lettuce leaf, then gnaw upon an apple core, have a taste of pumpkin, suck a grape, nibble at a carrot, push his little face right inside a ripe fig, eat some pear or a mouthful of stale cheese, or perhaps go the other way round. At the end he ate the pomegranate. He would take out a red seed, hold it between his paws, bite into it and drink the juice, while making tiny noises of delight.

And when at last he had finished, he would come over to Cecile to have his nose wiped. Then he would comb his whiskers with his paws and tidy up his fur.

After that they would both look at one another silently for a long time. Both were filled with the wonder of what they saw.

For a Guinea Pig is a most perfect thing, especially one like Jean-Pierre, whose nose was exactly the right color of pink, not too dark and not too light. Every one of his whiskers was just the right distance from the other, not too long and not too short. His fur was soft and shiny, every hair in place. And his little feet had the loveliest of tiny toenails. Most beautiful of all were his golden eyes, which were like a still pool reflecting a golden sunset. Cecile felt if only somehow she could get to the bottom of this pool, she would find there and understand all the things Jean-Pierre seemed to be trying to say to her.

And a little girl, too, is a most perfect thing, especially one like Cecile. For her dark hair was as fine and smooth as silk, her mouth as red as pomegranate seeds, and her face was as brown as an autumn leaf.

Most wonderful were her eyes, and Jean-Pierre felt that behind them lay all the things which Cecile seemed to be trying to say to him and which he could not understand.

'Oh, Jean-Pierre,' Cecile would sigh, 'why can't you talk to me ?'

But in Jean-Pierre's tiny ears it only sounded like the passing of the wind through the trees.

'Oh, Cecile,' Jean-Pierre cried, 'why can't you talk to me?'
But to Cecile it only sounded like a far-off twitter.

It wasn't at all that way with Bobi, the yellow dog, and Coco, the black cat. Cecile knew what they were thinking all the time. She knew when Bobi wanted to go out and when he wanted to come in. It was almost like talking. He had one kind of a bark when he had something up a tree, and another when he had something down a hole. He had a 'Let's-go-for-a-walk' bark and a 'Here-comes-a-stranger' bark. He could also say 'Isn't it a lovely day?' just by the way he waved his long yellow tail.

It was the same with Coco. You could tell when she was

pleased and you knew when she was angry. It was plain when she wanted to be loved and when she wanted to be alone. She never actually *said* anything, but she never left anyone in doubt that she did not want people to sit on the chair on which she liked to sleep. She also did not like water, or a cold wind, or smelly people, or to be disturbed when she was watching a mouse-hole.

Cecile somehow had never found herself wishing that she could talk to Bobi, or wondering what Coco was thinking as she lay with her feet tucked up under her. And she certainly had never thought of wanting to have a word with Gris-Gris, the rabbit.

With Jean-Pierre it was different. From the very first time she had laid eyes on him, she wanted to know what he was thinking as he looked up so eagerly into her face. And now that he was her very own and they could be together, she felt it a hundred times more strongly. Whenever she carried him about, she held his little warm body close to her cheek, to listen to the soft sounds he was making, hoping sometime she would understand. For it would be the most wonderful thing in the world to have a Guinea Pig to whom one could *tell* things, secrets and the like, sad things and happy things that one could not say to grown-ups or even one's school friends.

And then Jean-Pierre, at the same time, could tell her all he knew. Sometimes he looked to be so full of words to say that it seemed as though his sides would burst. They would be things that no little girl had ever heard before.

Once, Cecile's mother asked her, 'What on earth do you do down there in the cellar for hours with Jean-Pierre?'

Cecile replied, 'Nothing.' And then added, 'Oh, I wish, I wish, I wish Jean-Pierre could speak to me! Today he *almost* did.'

Cecile's mother said, 'Oh, darling, you know very well that animals can't speak.'

Cecile did not mind her mother saying this. It was just like all grown-ups who didn't understand. It only made her wish the harder.

Since it never ever came any closer than 'almost,' Cecile kept on wishing. The longer they were friends, the harder she wished.

She even took to adding her wish, silently, to the end of her prayers at night. When she was all finished with those she asked

God to bless (and after Mummy and Daddy came a long list of grandmothers, aunts, uncles, cousins and friends), and before she said her Amen, she would quickly think to herself *Oh, and please let Jean-Pierre talk to me.*

In the dark, in the corner of his cage on his little bed of straw, Jean-Pierre was doing the very same thing every night when he said his prayers. It took him longer to get to it because he had so many more of everyone than Cecile. He had brothers, sisters, aunts and uncles by the dozens, cousins by the hundreds and more grandparents than anyone could imagine. But when he had reached the end of the list, he would add, '*And, oh, please let Cecile talk to me.*'

And so the days passed.

ONE SUNDAY MORNING, which ought not to have been different from any other morning, Cecile woke up, sat up in bed and felt very odd. She felt special.

She felt most special.

That very same Sunday morning, and at the very same time, Jean-Pierre woke up in his little nest of straw. He lifted his pink nose from beneath his pink paws. He sniffed. He sneezed. And HE felt special.

He, too, felt *most* special.

Looking out of her window, Cecile saw the sun and the sea. The blue Mediterranean was shining as though it were covered with gold and diamonds. The sun had not yet climbed high into the sky. It seemed to be resting for a moment upon the edge of the water, so close it seemed to Cecile as though they were talking to one another.

She had never seen anything like this before. And the first thought that came to her was, *could this perhaps be the day that Jean-Pierre and I will be able to speak to one another?*

Each new morning she hoped that it might be, but this was the first morning ever when she felt as though it could really happen.

Jean-Pierre looked out of the window to the trees on the hillside. They were rustling and nodding and their branches were touching one another, as though they were holding hands and whispering together.

Jean-Pierre had never noticed this before, and he thought, *could this be the day, perhaps, when Cecile and I will be able to speak to one another?*

When Cecile got out of her bed she had a tingling all over and a peculiar feeling in her tummy.

Can you remember what it is like when you wake up in the morning and know that it is your birthday? Or Christmas? Or that at last the day has arrived when you will be going off on holiday to the seaside? That was how Cecile felt.

It wasn't her birthday. It wasn't Christmas. She wasn't going anywhere at all. But she was filled with excitement. She felt that if she gave a leap she would fly right out through the window. She did not do so because she had more sense. But the tingling all over and the feeling in her tummy told her that something tremendous might be going to happen that day.

Exactly the same thing was happening to Jean-Pierre, except that being a Guinea Pig, he felt it in different places.

With him it began with a kind of tickling in his nose. The tickling then ran between his ears and along his back, right down to the place where his tail ought to have been, if he had had one. Guinea Pigs, however, have no tails.

Then he sneezed four times and felt that if he gave a leap he could fly through the bars of his cage, out of the window, past the pump in the courtyard, over the roofs of the glass-houses and right to the top of the trees.

He didn't do so because he had more sense. But the tickling which had now spread all over him, even to his pink toes, and three more sneezes, told him also that something tremendous might be going to happen to him that day.

The water that morning in Cecile's bath looked like silver, and when it ran from the tap it sang a little song to her. The soap kept out of her eyes. She was dry in a jiffy. Her clothes seemed fairly to leap onto her back. Other times, Cecile was rather slow in dressing. It was that kind of day!

As Jean-Pierre set about giving his fur its morning clean, the sun crept through the door of the barn and across the floor, like a river of gold. Other times it took Jean-Pierre quite a while to comb the tangles out of his fur, put his whiskers right and clear the cobwebs from his eyes. Now everything went quickly. His coat was brushed as smooth as silk. His whiskers straightened. His eyes cleared. And before he knew it he was ready. That was the kind of day it was!

The day was all shivery with excitement, when everything seemed to be different to Cecile. Breakfast tasted better. The eggs were yellower. The toast crisper. The milk was sweeter.

Outside the house even the air seemed softer. The colors of all the flowers in the glass-houses were brighter, and the flowers themselves seemed to know something was going to happen, for

when Cecile looked in through the door at them they put their heads together as though they were whispering.

Sounds were not the same either. The church bells rang more joyously. The whistle of the train rushing past down by the sea seemed to say 'Farewell' more sadly. The birds in the woods sounded different. So did the cooing of the pigeons and the sighing of the wind.

As soon as Cecile had finished her breakfast, she ran to get Jean-Pierre and her feet hardly seemed to touch the ground. For whatever it was that would happen, she and Jean-Pierre must be together.

When she went into the barn and opened the door of his cage, he was waiting for her, and she saw at once how special he was, like everything else that special day.

For if his nose had been pink before, it was now twice as pink. And if his whiskers had been white before, they were twice as white now. And his coat shone and his golden eyes were as bright as though little fires burned within them.

Cecile took him in her hand and held him to her face. She whispered, 'Oh, Jean-Pierre. I feel as though something wonderful is going to happen to us today'.

Jean-Pierre did not understand a word, but he thought he almost did.

When he was close to her cheek he whispered in her ear, 'Oh, Cecile. I think something wonderful might be going to happen to us today.'

27

But it was still Guinea Pig Talk and Cecile didn't understand a word he said. But she thought she almost did.

So it must be going to take place soon.

Then they went out together to look for the place where it would be going to happen to them, whatever it was. Neither Cecile nor Jean-Pierre knew where to look, or what it was going to be, or how they would know.

They went down to the brook and waited. It sang happily as it tumbled downhill over the rocks. But nothing happened there.

They went up into the glen on the hill behind the glass-houses, where the pine trees rustled. They saw a grasshopper fiddling with its legs. But that was all. It didn't happen there.

They went off into the apple orchard and listened to the humming of the bees. An apple fell from a tree with a thud, and Bobi came rushing up and barked at it. But nothing else happened.

They passed beneath the grape arbor, slowly, with Cecile taking care not to step on the cracks of the stones of the walk, just in case. But it made no difference.

They went through the barn into the potting-shed and from there into the hothouse where the tiny seedlings of new flowers were just pushing green leaves above the dark earth in the boxes. They waited. The seedlings seemed to be full of joy to be above the earth at last, but that was all. It didn't happen there either.

They visited the different flowers, on the terraces out of doors, thinking perhaps that they might know the secret. But although before they had seemed to be whispering to one another, now they only turned silent and watchful.

Yet all through that strange morning, both Jean-Pierre and Cecile *knew* that this was the day for which they had both been longing, and that it must happen somewhere.

They went up into the attic, where Cecile was almost certain

it would have to be, because there were so many exciting things there. There were boxes and old newspapers, a chair with only three legs, a table slit down the middle, a spider who let himself down from the roof, and some broken toys with which Cecile didn't play any longer. They found a pair of shoes and an old hat and all sorts of other things no longer useful. It was dark, with only tiny bits of light shining through the cracks in the red tiles of the roof.

Cecile whispered, 'Shhh, Jean-Pierre. Don't make a sound,' and held his little warm body closer to her face. But after a while it was clear that it was not to be there either. All that took place was that the spider pulled himself up on his silken rope and went back into his hole under the roof.

They came downstairs again, into the hall, not knowing where to go now, for they had been to almost every place.

And then it happened!

Whoever would have thought that the secret was hidden within the old grandfather clock in the hall?

THE CLOCK WAS almost as old as the house, which was very old indeed. It was so tall it reached almost to the ceiling. Its face was large and round. Cecile always thought it was rather like a real face. It had a picture of the sun and the moon on it, which were like two eyes. In the middle were two holes into which you put the key to wind the clock and the striker. They were like a nose. And at the bottom there was a place which told you what day of the month it was, and this was like a little mouth. Whenever Cecile passed through the hall, she always felt as though the old clock was watching her.

Its tick was loud and clear. Its tock was even louder and clearer. But what was really loudest and clearest was when it struck the hour.

This was indeed a great effort. The clock was so old that it took a long time to get ready to strike. First it shook. Then it shivered. Then it buzzed. Then it whirred. Then it made a noise exactly like someone falling downstairs. And then at last it struck. 'Bong! Bong! Bong!'

Its voice was deep and could be heard all over the house and even down in the cellar.

When Cecile passed by that day, with Jean-Pierre still cuddled to her face, she felt as always that the clock was following her with its eyes. This time she stopped and turned around quickly to try to catch it.

And catch it she did.

The clock was watching her. But this time it was not only watching her, it was smiling at her. And not only was it smiling at her, but it seemed to be holding out its arms as though wishing she and Jean-Pierre would come closer.

Cecile went over to the clock, holding Jean-Pierre tightly. She stood on her tiptoes and looked up into its face so that if it did speak to her she would not miss a word.

First the clock said only, as all clocks do, 'Tick-tock, tick-tock.'

But then it changed and said, 'Tock-tick, tock-tick,' as clocks sometimes will if you start counting with the tock instead of with the tick.

And then, to their surprise, it said loud and clear:


'Tick-tock, tick-tock,
Speak to each other between twelve o'clock.
Tock-tick, tock-tick,
Between twelve o'clock,
You must be quick!'


It was happening at last. Cecile had understood every word that the clock had said.

And, cuddled in her hand, Jean-Pierre had also understood, just as though it had been speaking in Guinea Pig Talk.

At last the thing for which each had wished so hard was going to happen.

But what did the clock mean by *between* twelve o'clock? How could something be *between* twelve o'clock? It was either twelve o'clock or it wasn't. It could be before twelve or after twelve, but neither Cecile nor Jean-Pierre had ever heard of such a

thing as between twelve. How naughty of the clock to grant them their wish and then speak in riddles. They said the rhyme over to themselves and tried very hard to think what the clock had meant. . . .

'Tick-tock, tick-tock,
Speak to each other between twelve o'clock.
Tock-tick, tock-tick,
Between twelve o'clock,
You must be quick!'

They simply could not guess, and both looked up anxiously at the clock to see if perhaps it might have something more to say to them.

But it was silent for the moment and hid its face behind its hands, because it was about to strike the hour of eleven.

And, as you have heard, striking was a most serious matter for the grandfather clock, because everything inside it was so very old.

First it shook. Then it shivered. Then it buzzed. Then it whirred. Then came the noise like someone falling downstairs, and after that it began to strike.

'Bong! Bong! Bong!'

Cecile and Jean-Pierre counted, 'One. Two. Three.'

'Bong! Bong!'

'Four. Five.'

All of a sudden, Cecile gave a loud shriek, and at the same time Jean-Pierre gave a tiny shriek. For each, at the same moment, knew what the clock had been trying to tell them.

*Between* twelve o'clock must be the time between the first stroke and the last stroke of midday.

Count slowly! One—two—three—four—five—six—seven—eight—nine—ten—eleven—twelve.

They were to be allowed to speak to one another for no more than it would take you to count from one to twelve. That was why the clock had said, 'Be quick!'

Oh, dear! And at the same time, Oh, joy! How wonderful to be the only little girl and the only little Guinea Pig in the whole world to be allowed to talk to one another. But what would they say, or could they say, or did they want to say during the time the clock was striking twelve? Especially after they had been wanting to for so long, and had been saving up for hours and days and weeks and even a month?

It would have to be something most important. Or most secret. Or most exciting. Something each would never be able to forget.

It was now past eleven.

Each tick and each tock was bringing them closer to the magic moment that had been promised.

With a last look back at the grandfather clock, to make sure it had nothing more to tell them, Cecile hurried out of the hall and down the steps to the secret place in the cellar. It was just under the clock on the floor above, where they would be able to hear it strike, and that was where she wanted them to be. But, alas, there was not a great deal of time left to think of what to say.

Cecile thought, *Ought I to tell Jean-Pierre when my birthday is?*

Jean-Pierre thought, *Should I tell Cecile about the day I fell off the shelf in the pet shop and hurt my nose?*

Cecile wondered, *Should I tell Jean-Pierre I was first in school last week?*

Jean-Pierre questioned, *Ought I speak to Cecile about my father winning a Blue Ribbon at a Guinea Pig Show?*

Cecile asked herself, *Would Jean-Pierre like to hear about my cousin Robert, who lives in Paris, coming to stay with us at Christmas?*

Jean-Pierre worried, *Shall I tell Cecile that I am sometimes a little frightened of Coco?*

36

There were so many things they had to tell one another. Jean-Pierre could count up to ten before he had to start all over again, but there were many more things than that. And Cecile could count up to a thousand, because she was very good at counting, and there were more things than *that*.

What would YOU say to your Guinea Pig, or your dog, or your cat, or even your turtle or your goldfish, or your mouse, if you had no more than the time of counting slowly from one to twelve in which to say it?

And what would you like to have them tell *you*, if that was all the time they had to say it?

Down in the cellar Cecile put Jean-Pierre on his stone shelf. She cried, 'Soon, soon, Jean-Pierre! But what am I going to say to you? What *is it* you would like to know?'

And Jean-Pierre sat up and squeaked, 'Oh, Cecile, I have so many, many things to say to you. What is it YOU would most like to hear?'

But they could not understand one another—YET!

On Sundays, as a special treat, Jean-Pierre had his dinner at midday, just like the family. And now Cecile set about getting it for him. But she was so excited over what was going to happen that she hardly knew what she was doing, and became most mixed up.

She was so excited that instead of pumpkin slices, she gave him a banana. Instead of an apple, she gave him a turnip. Instead of pomegranate seeds, she fetched him a dog biscuit, kept in a sack for Bobi. She meant to feed him with some cabbage leaf and instead gave him a plate of sardines, put to one side for Coco the cat. And in place of his usual saucer of milk she poured out some red wine from an old bottle nearby in the cellar.

But Jean-Pierre did not mind. He didn't even notice. Actually, he wasn't hungry. He was too busy trying to decide what to say.

Usually, when Cecile was getting Jean-Pierre his dinner he would be sitting up on his hind legs, sniffing. This time he was lying flat on his tummy on the stone shelf with his eyes shut and his little pink paws over them, thinking.

Should he tell Cecile about an all-white cousin of his who had pink eyes? Ought he to let her know that sometimes when the window of the barn was left open, and the wind blew down from the north, he was cold? Or would she prefer to hear about an uncle of his who had almost gone to America once?

Cecile didn't even see whether Jean-Pierre was eating his meal, because she was always having to run upstairs and look at the hands on the face of the grandfather clock to see how near they were to twelve.

And the nearer they came, the harder she tried to find what to say to Jean-Pierre.

Ought she to tell him about the time she had cut her finger on a broken flower-pot, and the doctor had come and put in two stitches, and she hadn't cried? Would he care to hear about the day she had swum one hundred yards and won a diploma which was framed, and hung over her bed? Or would he prefer to know that when she grew up, Cecile was going to be either a nurse, or a teacher, or an artist, or a film star—she had not quite made up her mind which?

Cecile came rushing down the cellar steps. She was out of breath and almost in tears.

'Oh, Jean-Pierre,' she cried, 'it's only two minutes more to twelve and I still don't know what it is I want to tell you.'

Jean-Pierre didn't need to understand Cecile's words. He always knew what time it was by the feeling in the ends of his whiskers. He knew very well that there were only two minutes left to twelve, and he also knew that he had been unable to make up his mind what to tell Cecile when the time came.

Jean-Pierre took his paws from over his face and, opening his golden eyes, he looked into the gray ones of Cecile. He saw the tears there. If Guinea Pigs could cry, he too would have done so.

And now, upstairs, through the floor, they heard the grand-

father clock shake. Then it shivered. Then it buzzed. Then it whirred. Finally it made the noise like someone falling downstairs and then at last, they heard the deep, booming strike of the hour.

'Bong!' It was the first note of the magic moment between twelve.

And then, suddenly, Cecile didn't have to think any more of what it was she wanted to say. She knew!

She looked into the little browny face, with the pink nose, the white whiskers and the tiny ears, so fine you could almost see through them. She saw a poor little Guinea Pig, with a marking somewhat in the shape of a potato on his back, who wasn't really very pretty. But he was her very own.

And she cried, 'Oh, Jean-Pierre! I love you!'

Jean-Pierre looked into the brown face of Cecile. Two shining

tears still clung to the gray eyes and he no longer had to think what it was he wished to say to her. He also knew.

He saw a lonely little girl, who was really not all *that* pretty, for she had freckles and her nose turned up a little and her hair wasn't too tidy, but she was his very own and they belonged to one another.

'Oh, Cecile!' he cried, 'I love you!'

And then each repeated to one another, 'I love you!'

That was all they said, while upstairs the grandfather clock boomed away the last strokes.

Each had understood. Each had warmed the heart of the other. For the words were the most beautiful ones that a little girl could say to a tiny Guinea Pig. And the words were quite the most beautiful ones that a tiny Guinea Pig could say to a little girl.

In fact they were the most beautiful words that anyone could ever speak to anyone, anywhere, anytime. They were words that anyone could understand, no matter in what language they were spoken.

Cecile picked up Jean-Pierre and, cuddling him under her chin, went upstairs into the hall to say 'thank you' to the grandfather clock.

Cecile stood once more on tiptoes and held Jean-Pierre up to where the clock could see him with the sun and the moon of its eyes, and whispered, 'Thank you!'

The grandfather clock replied:

> 'Tick-tock, tick-tock,
> You spoke to each other between twelve o'clock.
> Tock-tick, tock-tick,
> It's going on One,
> Tick-tock, tick-tock,
> Well done! Well done!'

Cecile's mother came out of the kitchen and said, 'What on earth are you doing, Cecile, holding poor Jean-Pierre up to the clock like that?'

'Nothing,' said Cecile.

But it had been really something, and she felt happier than she ever had in her life before as the clock repeated:

'Tick-tock, tick-tock,
You spoke to each other
Between twelve o'clock.
Tock-tick, tock-tick,
It's going on One,
Tick-tock, tick-tock,
Well done! Well done!'